Guy Parker-Rees

DYLAN

THE DOCTOR

Hello, I'm Dotty Bug.
Let's follow along with the story!

Cartwheel Books
An imprint of Scholastic Inc.

When it's a sunny day,
Dylan's ready to play.

But what sort of day was it today?
A quiet, stay-at-home day?

No way!

Today was a
Making-Everyone-Better Day!

So Dylan dashed into
his kennel, and found . . .

. . . his doctor's bag!

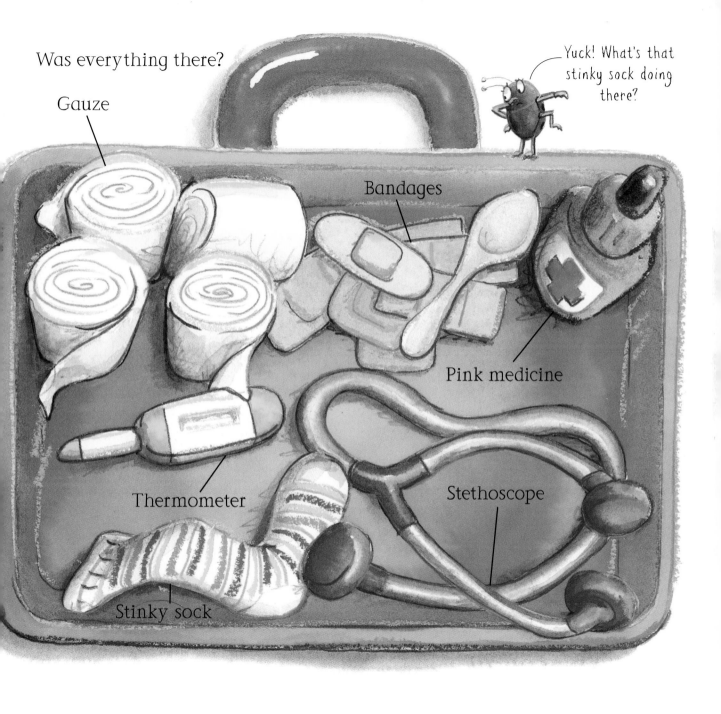

Doctor Dylan zoomed down the path.

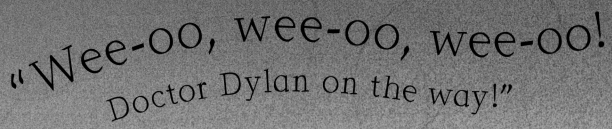

"Wee-oo, wee-oo, wee-oo!
Doctor Dylan on the way!"

Suddenly, he heard a cry.

Can YOU go
wee-oo, too?

It was Kala Cat.

"What's the matter, Kala Cat?"

"I've hurt my head, Doctor.
And my shoulders, knees, and toes."

"Oh, no!" said Doctor Dylan.

"You've got Head-Shoulders-Knees-and-Toes-Itis."

He bandaged her up right away.

"Thank you, Doctor,"
said Kala Cat. "That's much better."

Doctor Dylan set off again.

"Wee-oo, wee-oo, wee-oo!
Doctor Dylan on the way!"

Suddenly, he heard a noise.

It was Ozzy Otter!

"What's the matter, Ozzy Otter?"

"My tail feels too flappy!"

"Oh, no!" said Doctor Dylan.

"You've got Floppy-Wobble Fever."

He took Ozzy Otter's temperature and put three bandages on his tail.

Do YOU ever need a bandage?

"Thank you, Doctor!" said Ozzy Otter.

"I'm feeling less flappy already."

Doctor Dylan was just about to set off
again when Kala Cat came running.
"Doctor! Quick! It's Bitsy Chick! And it's an
EMERGENCY!"

Bitsy Chick
didn't look very well.
"What's the matter,
Bitsy Chick?"

"Cheep!" said Bitsy Chick,
but it was a very un-chirpy cheep.
"She needs to go to my hospital,
right away," said Doctor Dylan.

So they all made an
extra-loud ambulance noise:

"Wee-oo, wee-oo, wee-oo!"

and they rushed Bitsy Chick
back to Dylan's kennel.

Have YOU ever been
in a hospital?

"What she needs," said Doctor Dylan,
"is lots of loving care."

So he fluffed up a pillow,
and tucked her in with a blanket,
and gave her lots of pink medicine
and lots and lots of love.

Bitsy Chick was soon feeling much better.

That looks comfy.

When the other two saw Bitsy Chick
getting so much fuss, they decided
that they felt really bad, too.
"We need **lots** of loving care as well,
Doctor Dylan!" they said.

Do YOU like lots of
loving care, too?

So now Doctor Dylan had to look after everyone.

He fluffed up everyone's pillows,
and gave everyone blankets,

and listened to everyone's chest,
and gave everyone pink medicine.

Then Ozzy Otter needed a drink,
so Doctor Dylan gave him some juice.

And Kala Cat was hungry,
so Doctor Dylan brought her
some marshmallows.

And Bitsy Chick needed even
more loving care, so
Doctor Dylan made her a
get-well-soon card
(with glitter) to cheer her up.

That's pretty.

Then he sang everyone a song,
and did a dance,

and read them all a story.

At long last, Doctor Dylan said . . .

"Oh, no!" said the others.
"Who's going to take care of Doctor Dylan?"

Poor Doctor Dylan!

"We all are!"

said Doctor Kala Cat,
Doctor Bitsy Chick,
and Nurse Ozzy Otter.

Do YOU like looking after people?

And they gave him
lots and lots of the
most loving care ever!

For Dylan,

and a big thank you to the
hugely creative Alison and Zoë.

Dylan the Doctor was first published in the UK by Alison Green
Books, an imprint of Scholastic Children's Books, in 2016.

ISBN 978-1-338-25580-5

10 9 8 7 6 5 4 3 2 1   18 19 20 21 22

Printed in Malaysia   108
This edition first printing, August 2018